For Mom, Cindy, and Elieanna,
and also for Franny

First edition 2008

Library of Congress Cataloging-in-Publication Data is available.

Library of Congress Catalog Card Number pending

ISBN 978-0-7636-3072-0

2 4 6 8 10 9 7 5 3 1

Printed in China

This book was typeset in Malonia Voigo.
The illustrations were done in oil.

Candlewick Press
2067 Massachusetts Avenue
Cambridge, Massachusetts 02140

visit us at www.candlewick.com

DUCK

Randy Cecil

CANDLEWICK PRESS
CAMBRIDGE, MASSACHUSETTS

Duck was a carousel animal who longed to fly. She knew her carved wooden wings were not made for flying. But she couldn't stop thinking about it, even when the carousel was whirling around.

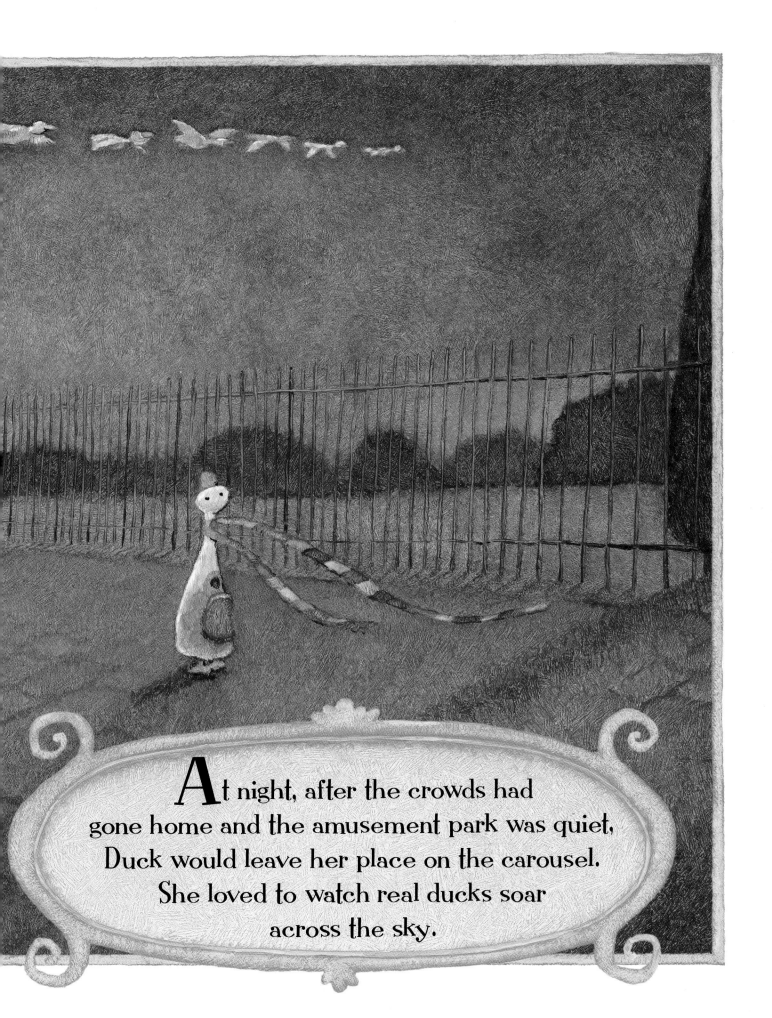

At night, after the crowds had
gone home and the amusement park was quiet,
Duck would leave her place on the carousel.
She loved to watch real ducks soar
across the sky.

She would lie down on the cobblestones and look up at the stars. She wondered how close flying ducks could get to the stars.

And when Duck fell asleep,
she dreamed she was among them.

Then one spring day,
everything changed. A little lost duckling
ambled through the front gate and
walked right up to Duck.

W hat's this? wondered Duck.
It had a bill like a duck and feet like a duck.
But she had never seen such a small duck before,
or one so yellow and fuzzy.

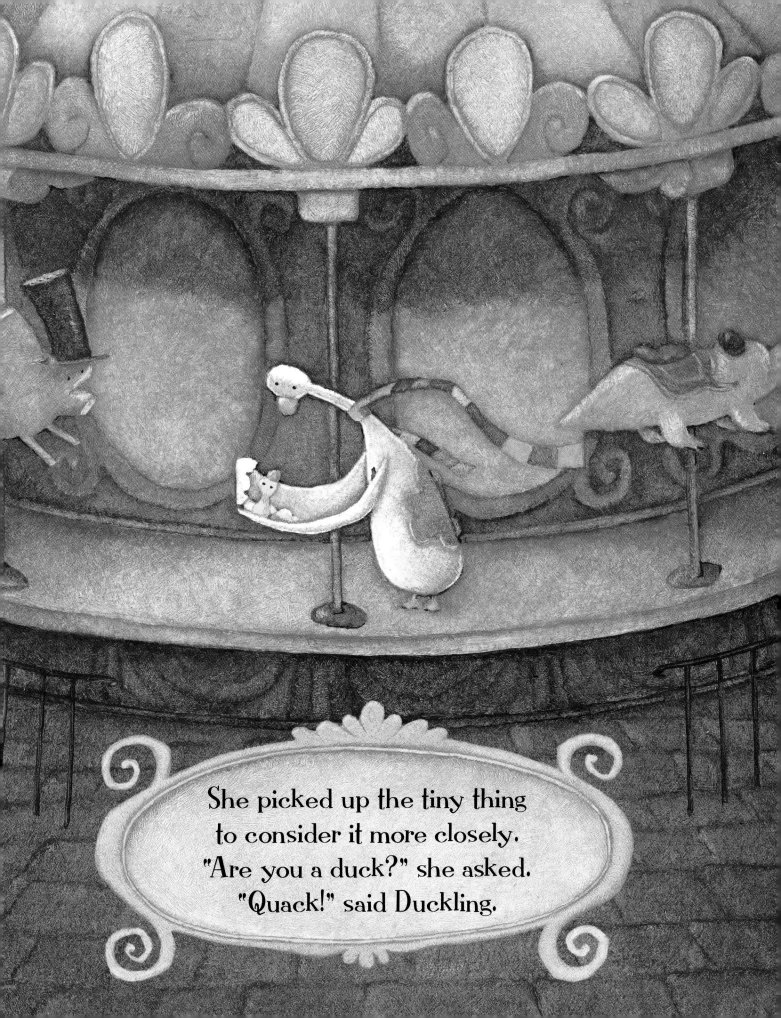

She picked up the tiny thing
to consider it more closely.
"Are you a duck?" she asked.
"Quack!" said Duckling.

From that moment on, Duck and Duckling were always together.

They laughed together.

They played together.

They even dreamed the same dreams together.

As time passed, Duckling's yellow fuzz turned
into beautiful white feathers and his little wings
began to look like flying ducks' wings.
Soon he was mastering real duck things like
shoveling through the mud for bugs.

But he showed no signs of flying.
If Duckling was ever going to fly, Duck decided
she would have to teach him.

So they began Duckling's training.

In the mornings,
they worked on jumping.
A good jump is
essential for takeoff.

Next came flapping
practice. Anyone will
tell you how important
flapping is to flying.

Then Duck would help
Duckling climb up
on her back so Duckling
could feel the wind
on his wings as
the carousel turned.

There were wonderful
moments when
it looked like Duckling
might take off and
fly straight up to
the clouds.

But he never quite did.

Duck knew it was time to find the ones who
could teach Duckling what she could not.

So Duck strapped Duckling tightly to her back with
her scarf and set off in search of real ducks.

She walked and walked. Then suddenly she saw them — a group of ducks floating in a stream.

"Now remember to be polite," she said to Duckling as she straightened some of his new feathers. "You're going to do fine."

But when she looked for the ducks again, they were gone.

"Wait!" Duck cried as she raced to the top
of a hill. The real flying ducks were high in the sky,
heading south. What if they never found them again?
How would Duckling learn to fly?

Then something magical happened.

They were flying! Sort of.

Duckling was flying, but actually they were
sinking more than they were flying.
Duck was just too heavy for Duckling.

As they sank lower and lower,
Duck realized what she had to do.

She freed herself from the scarf.
Right away, Duckling went up.

And Duck went down.

Up, up, up went Duckling.
Down, down, down went Duck.

Duck kept going until she hit the ground and skidded to a stop. She looked up just in time to see Duckling taking his place among the other real ducks.

A moment later they were gone.

Duck limped back home to the amusement park,
alone and scarfless, to face the long winter ahead.

And a long winter it was.

It snowed and snowed.

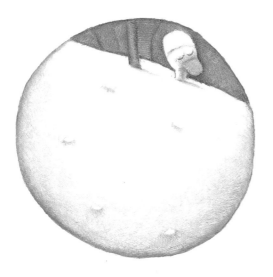

It snowed so much,
Duck almost disappeared.

But finally, spring returned.
The snow melted away, and Duck was
awakened by the bright sun.

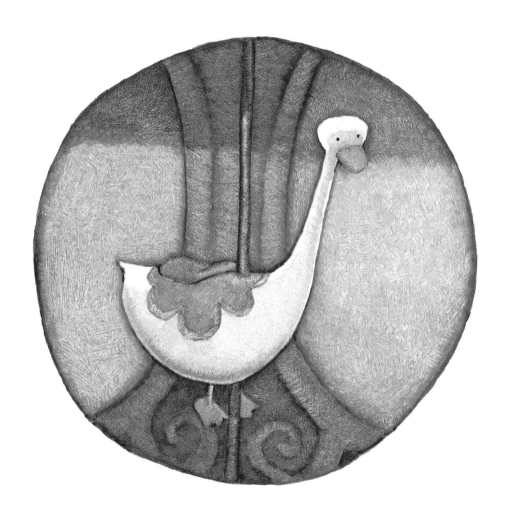

The real ducks were returning, too. But Duck
no longer wanted to watch them fly. It was flying
that had taken Duckling away from her.

Duck sat at the edge of
the carousel and lowered her head.
Then, out of the corner of her eye,
she saw something. . . .

It was a real flying duck. But not just any duck. This one was wearing Duck's scarf and flying right toward her. "Duckling!" she cried. "Quack!" said Duckling.

"Let me look at you!" said Duck. "You're all grown up." Duckling preened as Duck patted his head and smoothed his tail feathers.

All that day they
laughed together

and played together,

just as they had so many times before.

As night came, Duckling prepared
to leave again with his flock. But first, Duckling
helped Duck climb up on his back.

And finally, Duck knew what it was to fly.

JP   Cecil, Randy.

Duck.